Poems Your Parents Won't Lik

Johnny 'Mogs' Morris

Edited by Black Pear Press

First published in September 2017 by Black Pear Press
www.blackpear.net

ISBN 978-1-910322-47-5

Cover Illustration by Claudia Swingewood-Hughes
Art and Design Centre—Stourbridge College

Rear Cover Illustration by Sue Morris

Black Pear Press

Introduction

Mogs never intended to write poetry for children, he just wrote poems that he found amusing. It was only when friends suggested younger readers might enjoy them he decided to produce a book.

Unfortunately he has a strange sense of humour so some of his poems are about rather horrible things like bogies and farts. This may mean that some parents won't want their kids to read them, but hey, we don't always do what our parents tell us to do.

To make the book even more fun, Mogs asked a bunch of talented artists to do some rather brilliant illustrations. So if you don't like the poems, you'll love the pictures!

Dedication

I would like to dedicate this book to children of all ages who find poetry dull and boring, as I did when I was at school. I hope it encourages them to read more, and even to write their own poems.

Other Writers' Say:

"'Poems Your Parents Won't Like' is a delightful first collection of poems, silly, even ridiculous, but very funny and cleverly written, from Johnny 'Mogs' Morris. A treasure trove providing answers to such questions as: 'Why do giraffes wear turtle necks?' 'Who is the witch with filthy habits?' 'Do wasps cry?' Gently introducing aliens, a scary canary, a vegetarian spider and the perils of eating chocolate cake, together with a smattering of bogies and a faint scent of foul smells, this book will have you laughing whether you are six or sixty."—Maggie Doyle
Worcestershire Poet Laureate Emeritus

"If you are glum and feeling grey
Read a poem to cheer your day.
Johnny Morris; known as Mogs
Creates laughter about cats and dogs,
Sharks and wasps and even birds
Are subjects of poetic words.
There's a verse that is a charmer
As it features a banana!
Enjoy this book and all the rhymes
Will make you giggle many times!"
—Mark Billen

"Mogs is one of the most talented humourists and engaging performance poets in the Midlands whose understated delivery lets his poetry speak for itself. I've seen him many, many times and he has always connected with his audience in ways that most other poets can only dream about. If you like poetry that will put a smile on your face, you'll certainly enjoy his book."—
Fergus McGonigal
Worcestershire Poet Laureate 2014-2015

Contents

Dung Beetle

It's a dirty job, I know it is,
But someone has to do it,
You can't leave a pile just steaming there,
'Cus someone might walk through it.

Some say that I'm the lowest of the low,
But I don't care what people think,
'Cus if stuff was left just where it fell,
The place would really stink.

So I roll it up into nice big balls
And shift it if I can,
I'm a dung beetle and always have
A big job on my hands.

As a career it isn't much,
But I don't really care,
That I've started at the bottom
And like as not, I will stay there.

Folks should show me more respect,
'Cus the job I do is super,
It means they can do things where they want,
And I'll be their pooper-scooper.

I'm one of nature's street cleaners,
As a job you cannot beat it,
'Cus I get to take work home with me,
And then I get to eat it.

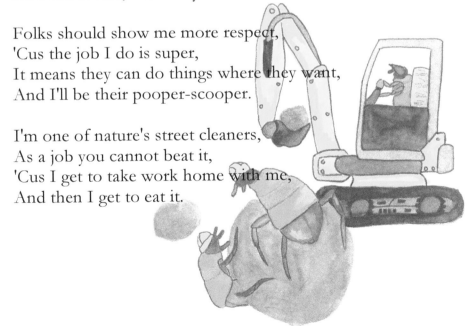

Dung Beetle—Adam Morris

Bogey Boy

Everybody called him 'Bogey Boy',
It's not the name his mother chose,
But he was the boy who always had
His finger firmly up his nose.

His mom would often warn him,
"Your nose isn't there to pick,
If you keep shoving your finger up,
One day, it will surely stick."

Well Bogey Boy didn't listen,
He said, "Nose picking is fun,
There's always a new bogey there,
Look, I've just found another one."

Each day as Bogey Boy woke up,
There was one thing that he'd do,
He'd insert a digit up his nose,
And what he pulled out, he'd chew.

Then one fateful day he put it up,
And there, quite firm it stuck,
For days the doctors stood and stared;
Their heads they gravely shook.

Bogey Boy—Jonathan Morris

For months that's where his digit remained,
And by everyone he was teased,
Until one day his life was changed,
It popped out as he sneezed!

So Bogey Boy had his finger back,
He said, "Well that's a great relief.
"I'll pick bogies from my nose no more,
"I'll pick them from my handkerchief."

Spike

My name is Spike,
I go where I like,
I rummage round in rubbish bins.
All through the day
In bed I stay,
It's at night when my day begins.

Yes, my name is Spike,
I can't ride a bike,
And some think my diet is quite sickly,
It's slugs that I eat.
If ever we meet,
I'll roll into a ball and be prickly.

Yes, my name is Spike,
Warm weather I like,
I've no fur and my skin is thin.
In winter I keep
In bed, fast asleep,
But come spring I'll be back in your bin.

Spike—Claudia Swingewood-Hughes

Sock Monster—Adam Morris

Sock Monster

There's a sock monster loose in my house,
Of that I am really quite sure,
He lurks there in my washing machine,
And I know what he waits for.

Yes, even though I've never seen him,
He's there somewhere, there's no doubt,
And so I know my socks aren't safe.
Watch out! There's a sock monster about!

He skulks and prowls, stays out of sight.
He hides in the gloom and the dark,
He has no pity, stalking his prey,
Like a big scary sock-scoffing shark.

Just when I thought it might be safe
To go back in the washing machine,
As the spin-cycle comes to an end,
I can tell, once again, he has been.

'Cus as I begin to put socks together
Into pairs, from the tangled mix,
I come across one all on its own,
Then I know, he's been up to his tricks.

I wonder, sometimes, why does he do it?
Why's the sock monster mean?
He sits and watches me put them in,
And only eats my socks when they're clean.

He only takes one, never a pair,
And not any I've just had my feet in.
Do you think somewhere up in sock heaven
Are the soles of the socks he has eaten.

Well I try to be philosophical now,
When he takes one, I no longer care,
I don't think, I'm left with one useless sock,
But half of a brand new odd pair.

To Bee

Oh how I would like to be,
A busy buzzing bumble bee,
Live somewhere down by the sea,
And run an insect B&B.
My bumble bee wife and me,
In our seaside sanctuary,
Where every wasp, fly or flea,
Could be just where they want to be.

Bee—Jonathan Morris

Monk

There once was a greedy fat monk,
Who ate burgers and all kinds of junk,
He had a bad habit,
If he saw food, he'd grab it,
Then he'd claim that his habit had shrunk.

Monk—Georgia Cook

Basking Shark

I am a harmless basking shark,
My most favourite thing is basking,
So when the basking weather comes,
Just once do I need asking
To go out with my basking mates,
And spend the whole day basking,
Because you can't be sure how long
The basking weather's lasting.

The other sharks are not like us,
You'll never see them basking,
They rush about just eating folk,
We don't do stuff that's taxing.
Great whites are great at being white,
Hammerheads knock nails and tacks in,
Loan sharks don't like company,
And basking sharks like basking.

If a great white sees a swimming bloke,
For no reason he attacks him,
But if he swims by us we say,
"Let's chill, and do some basking."
So be warned, if swimming in the sea
You find a shark you think is basking.
Make quite sure it's a basking shark,
Not a great white just relaxing.

Basking Shark—Adam Morris

Dodo—Jon Shariat

What Do Dodos Do?

In 1598 Dutch sailors were the first people to ever see a Dodo on the island of Mauritius.
This is an extract from their report.

It's not so much what the Dodo do,
It's more a case of what the Dodo don't.
Do they fly? Did they ever try?
Did they find they could, and now just won't?

Do the Dodo swim like the penguins do?
Did they try it once and get deterred?
Well how do they avoid their predators,
If they're a swimless, flightless bird?

Do Dodos taste really horrible?
Are they extremely tough to chew?
Do they fight like Teenage Ninja Dodos
Trained in Karate and Kung-Fu?

Is the Dodo a master of disguise?
Can they just disappear from view?
When cornered by a big hungry thing,
How do Dodos get out of the doo-doo?

Do Dodos do a distracting dance?
Is there a ferocious Dodo roar?
Do they dig a hole to keep them safe?
Are they poisonous? I'm not really sure.

Do the Dodo climb up into trees?
Are they nimble and very fast?
From what I've seen them do so far,
I don't think they're going to last.

'Cus when threatened, Dodos' negotiate,
They will discuss things nervously,
The last thing you hear a Dodo say
Is, "Please, do…do…don't eat me!"

Primates

My mates
Are primates,
They hang about in trees
My mates
Are primates,
My mates are chimpanzees.

My mates
Are primates,
Gibbons and monkeys too.
My mates
Are primates,
I do have quite a few.

My mates
Are primates,
Many sizes, many shapes,
My mates
Are primates,
Gorillas and great apes.

My mates
Are primates,
There's so many different sorts.
My mates
Are primates,
Some are tall and some are short.

My mates
Are primates,
They jump and swing and climb.
My mates
Are primates,
They are fit and in their prime.

My mates
Are primates,
Some of them live in the zoo.
My mates
Are primates,
One of my mates looks like you.

Primates—Adam Morris

10

Why Do Farts Smell?

There's one question many ponder,
On one issue, great minds dwell,
More than 'the meaning of life' itself,
They all wonder; why do farts smell?

One of life's unanswered questions,
It's still an unsolved mystery,
For years science has been baffled,
But the answer is clear to me.

'Cus as you can't feel or see them,
Your sense of sight and touch won't work,
And so if you couldn't smell a fart,
How'd you know where one might lurk?

If not for a nasal warning,
You'd sit somewhere unaware,
Oblivious to the danger
When someone had dropped one there.

So making farts aromatic,
Is just nature's unpleasant way
To warn of approaching gases,
And give you time to run away.

Why Do Farts Smell?
  —*Adam Morris*

Big Jim—Jon Shariat

Big Jim

Big Jim
Is tall and slim,
There's no one quite as tall as him,
The clouds are what his head is in,
Right there, up where the air is thin.

Small Pat
Is short and fat,
Jim's knees are level with her hat,
He's still much taller than poor Pat
When she's stood up and Jim is sat.

Big Jim
Is long of limb,
They dug a hole to stand him in,
And now Pat's knees are by Jim's chin,
And her head's up where Jim's hair is thin!

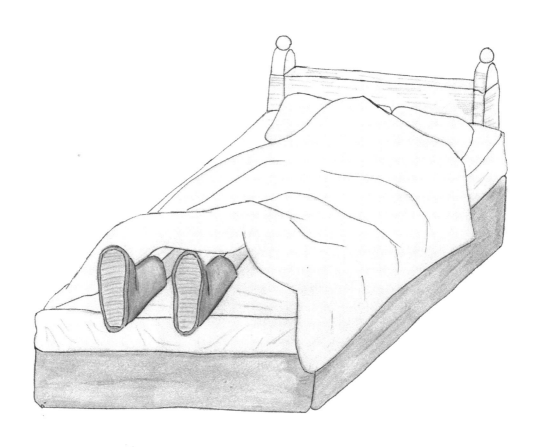

Welly-gogs—Adam Morris

Welly-gogs

I like to wear my welly-gogs,
People often ask me why.
Well, I think they look rather neat,
And keep my feet warm and dry.

I like to wear my welly-gogs,
Doesn't matter, come rain or shine,
The problem with my welly-gogs
Is actually, they're not mine.

I don't own any welly-gogs,
And when I ask my mother,
She says that when I need a pair,
I can lend them off my brother.

I always wear his welly-gogs,
Whenever he's not about,
'Cus if he sees me wearing them,
He shouts, "Oy! Get your feet out!"

They're rather small, these welly-gogs,
Though they fit my brother a treat,
I often struggle to get them on,
He must have really tiny feet.

Sometimes I sleep in welly-gogs,
When they hear, most people scoff,
But once I've got my wellies on,
Sometimes they just won't come off!

There's a hole now, in my welly-gogs,
That's no good when in a puddle,
'Cus I find some water will get in,
And also lots of mud'll.

I once had some lovely welly-gogs,
Made of rubber, a shiny black,
I no longer wear those welly-gogs,
'Cus my brother has had them back.

Trainee Witch—Jonathan Morris

Trainee Witch

She flies through the air with the greatest of ease,
She is one of the witch's oldest trainees.
She'll sit with her cat as she flies on her broom,
Once she's parked her big bum there isn't much room.
Quite often her face, with a cackle distorts,
As she picks at her nose and the scabs on her warts.
She'll swear and she'll curse, and utter her spells,
And lift a leg slightly to sneak out foul smells.

She flies through the air with the greatest of ease,
Her face is bright green, teeth as yellow as cheese.
She's rather unpleasant and does dreadful things,
Plucks the eyes out of newts, relieves bats of their
    wings.
On All Hallows Eve her cauldron will bubble,
While she and her mates are all out causing trouble,
She'll bang on folks' doors and demand tricks and
    treats,
All night she will prowl up and down empty streets.

She flies through the air with the greatest of ease,
Wears long pantaloons that come down to her knees,
Because she has found now that she's getting old,
When she's on her broomstick her bottom gets cold.
She's ever so spiteful; she's not very nice,
Turned my brother and me into newts once or twice,
She's stinky and mean, and yet I do love her,
She may be a cruel witch, but still, she's my mother.

Scary Canary—Jonathan Morris

Scary Canary

He sits there in his birdcage
With that mean look in his eye,
Unblinking, glaring, staring,
At ev'ry poor sod passing by.
With that brightly coloured plumage
Like a gaudy, scowling fairy.
He's a nuisance, he's a menace,
He is a scary canary.

He sits there, in near silence,
Then spits out a spiteful word,
You dare not go too close to him,
He's one vindictive bird.
Everyone's intimidated,
He's unpleasant and contrary,
It's best that you don't argue with
The mean scary canary.

He will stand there by his mirror,
And outstare his reflection,
He is cold, he is uncaring,
Spurns any kind of affection.
His beak is sharp and lethal,
He insanely dings his bell,
Even the cats avoid him,
The scary canary from hell!

You are really never safe,
He may be locked up in a cage,
But he sits with cold resentment
And simmering canary rage.
So if ever you are passing,
Take care, you should be wary,
It's best to keep your distance
From the scary canary.

The Spider And The Fly—Adam Morris

The Spider And The Fly

Said the spider to the fly,
"Why not come and sit right here?
I'm old, my legs are spindly,
You have nothing here to fear."

"My eyesight now, is fading,
My powers are on the ebb,
No longer do I have the spit
To spin any kind of web."

"I'm now a vegetarian,
And I like all kinds of veggies,
I live on nut roast casserole
With sprouts and 'tater wedges."

"My fly eating days are over,
No more houseflies will I throttle,
Yes I am on the wagon,
At last I'm off the bluebottle."

"So won't you sit beside me?
Come and talk with me a while,
Cross my heart and hope to die
I think eating flies is vile."

Said the fly to the spider,
"I'm sorry, but I don't believe
That you've changed your spider ways,
I think you mean but to deceive."

"'Cus I've just been in your larder,
And I had a good look round,
A safe distance I'll be keeping,
While I tell you what I found."

"There hung a sticky Kleenex,
Where my mates met their demise,
All stuck there; so I know your words
Are all just a tissue of flies!"

That Funny Woman

That funny woman, I'm not really sure
Why she is always there hanging around,
I find she turns up no matter the time,
If I move, or I make the slightest sound.

That funny woman, how does she do it?
She is always there whenever I wake,
I open my eyes; she scares me to death,
For goodness sake woman, give me a break!

That funny woman keeps talking to me,
The way she speaks, I think she's a nutter,
It's all funny noises, no language I know,
I can't understand a word she utters.

That funny woman, she gets on my nerves,
Though I suppose that I shouldn't be rude,
She always comes running when I call out
Wiping my bottom and giving me food.

That funny woman keeps picking me up,
I must say that it does annoy me.
Sometimes I catch her just sitting and staring,
She is weird! I wonder who she could be?!

That funny woman's always messing with me,
Mopping up sick, rubbing stuff on my bum,
Don't know who she is, but I've heard people talk,
That funny woman, they say, is my mum.

That Funny Woman—Naomi Reed

Snow

Snow is lovely.
Snow is nice.
Snow is wet and
Cold as ice.

Snow makes snowmen
And snowballs.
Snow is silent
As it falls.

I play in snow
When it's outside.
It makes me slip,
It makes me slide.

Snow collects in
Every corner.
I wish that snow
Was slightly warmer.

I wrap up warm
Each time it snows,
But still I get
Cold hands and toes.

Playing in snow
Just can't be beat.
It's worth cold fingers
And icy feet.

Grown-ups hate it,
That much I know.
But I wonder if
They've played in snow.

So much snow fell
Yesterday,
They've closed the school.
Hip-hip-hooray!

Snow illustrations
—Robyn Johnson

What Is The Point Of Grass?

So what is the point of grass then?
It's there, everywhere that I go,
It sprawls out in my back garden,
All it seems to do there is grow.

It gets longer all through the summer,
In winter, it never stops growing,
It sneaks up while you're not looking,
'Til Mum says, "The grass needs mowing."

Does it actually serve any purpose?
Do we need it to cover the ground?
Does it do anything but lie there
Making a faint 'growing sound'?

Everybody has a lawn with grass on,
If it didn't exist, would it hurt?
Can't nature find something better
That won't grow and gather the dirt?

Cats think that our lawn's a toilet,
It's where squirrels all bury their nuts,
If Dad doesn't trim it every day,
Mum just looks at it and tuts.

I can't walk on it barefooted,
The daisies attract wasps and bees,
It's full of red ants, and flesh-eating worms,
When Dad cuts it, it makes me sneeze.

If I sit on it, it stains my trousers,
If I eat it, it will make me sick.
Stuff handfuls down my sister's pants
She tends to go off me quite quick.

It grows up hills and in valleys,
It's a devil to keep the stuff clean,
It's spread all over the countryside.
Everywhere's that naff shade of green.

There are lots of blokes like my dad,
Who take out their mower each day,
To fight that long losing battle
To keep that green stuff at bay.

So what is the point of grass then?
To ban it, perhaps would be drastic,
But Dad says his life would be better
If grass was made out of plastic.

What Is The Point Of Grass?—Adam Morris

Pear

Once I had a pear,
A pear beyond compare,
Then I got another pear,
And so I had a pair.
But then I broke a pear,
And I was in despair.
I sent it for repair,
And once more I have a pair.

Pear—Claudia Swingewood-Hughes

Ode To A Scarecrow—Naomi Reed

Ode To A Scarecrow

Oh scarecrow stood in fields of corn,
You're standing there all day
Come rain or shine, with arms outstretched,
You scare the birds away.

Baa-baa Black Sheep—Jon Shariat

Baa-baa Black Sheep

Baa-baa black sheep
Have you any wool?
But in a different colour,
Because black is far too dull.
It's OK for balaclavas
For bank-robbers and SAS,
But black is so depressing
And won't really match my dress.

You seem to have a lot of mates,
But their fleece is somewhat plain,
It's a rather dingy shade of white
And everyone is just the same.
I've seen knitwear in bright colours,
Jumpers red and green and blue,
So where did they get the wool from?
Well it obviously wasn't ewe.

Baa-baa Black Sheep
—Robyn Johnson

Silly Sausage

I am a silly sausage,
The things I dreamt I'd do,
I suppose I should've realised,
Sausage dreams just don't come true.
I've done so little with my life,
Though the plans I had were grand,
But all I did was procrastinate,
And this banger's plans went bang.

Now from somewhere in the kitchen,
A poor silly sausage screams,
Prostrate upon a paper plate
And covered in hot baked beans.
It's no way to end your sausage days,
Lying on a breakfast plate,
I should've done more with my life,
But alas it's now too late.

Silly Sausage—Adam Morris

Kangaroo

Myth has it that the word 'kangaroo' in Aboriginal means 'I don't know'. So when the first Europeans landed in Australia and asked the locals what the big hopping animal was called they replied 'kangaroo' because they hadn't got a name for it.

I don't know what I am. Do you?
Some say that I'm a kangaroo.
I'm not too sure if that is true.
What is a kangaroo?

I am under no illusion,
That after all of the confusion,
Folks will jump to the conclusion,
That I am a kangaroo.

The front pocket is standard issue,
It's where I keep my phone and tissue,
If you saw it I bet you'd wish you
Were also a kangaroo.

Kangaroo
—Jonathan Morris

A pocket's good when you jump about,
It keeps things safe, there is no doubt,
But with short arms I can't get stuff out,
That's a problem for a kangaroo.

If there are places I need to pop,
Like to the water hole or shop,
I don't walk there, no, I just hop,
It's what you do as a kangaroo.

In the animal world I'm unique,
Folk say that I'm some kind of freak,
But I think I look rather chic,
Because I'm a kangaroo.

The word 'kangaroo', means – 'I don't know'.
And school was a place I didn't go,
I don't know what things are and so
Everything's a kangaroo.

My Dog Knows

My dog knows when I am angry,
My dog knows when I'm upset,
He knows not to lie on furniture,
When he comes in soaking wet.

My dog knows that my flowerbed
Is not the place to bury bones.
He knows not to chew my slippers,
TV-remote or mobile phones.

My dog knows when I am sleeping
He should be as quiet as a mouse,
When I'm out he knows not to leave
Little messages 'round the house.

My dog knows when we're out walking
There are things he should not do,
Like pick a fight with bigger dogs,
Or roll about in cow poo.

My dog knows that it's not pleasant,
The places some dogs put their nose,
It's not nice to sniff dogs' bottoms.
He shouldn't do that, my dog knows.

My dog knows when people visit,
He should keep still, behaving well,
And not rush round like a loony,
And sneak out the odd foul smell.

My dog knows, don't drink from toilets.
Or rummage through my shopping.
There's lots of things he shouldn't do,
My dog knows, but it doesn't stop him!

My Dog Knows—Jonathan Morris

Mockingbird

Mockingbird, oh mockingbird,
I hear you in your tree,
Perched high up in the branches
You sit there mocking me.

Mockingbird, oh mockingbird,
You copy everything,
To my song you will listen,
And then my song you sing.

Mockingbird, oh mockingbird,
No wonder you're alone.
You steal the songs of every bird,
Have you got none of your own?

Mockingbird, oh mockingbird,
You spend your whole life mocking,
You don't care who you upset,
Your attitude is shocking.

Mockingbird, oh mockingbird,
Take care, because I've heard,
It is no longer such a crime
To kill a mockingbird!

Mockingbird—Naomi Reed

I'm Sure I Was Abducted By Aliens—Jonathan Morris

I'm Sure I Was Abducted By Aliens

There were lights in the sky, and a strange eerie hum,
When fellows just three feet tall,
Appeared from nowhere and whisked me away,
The night the aliens came to call.
They strapped me down tight to a cold table top
In their spaceship, in space, as they flew,
And with long metal probes and many a strange thing
They did what aliens do.
They prodded and poked for quite a long time,
Made beeps and flapped big pointy ears.
Next thing I recall I was lay in a field,
And my 'friends' had just disappeared.
But I know what it is some people will say,
That it's a lie, or was just a dream.
But my adventure was real; of that I'm quite sure,
'Cus I'm no longer as once I had been.
I now have these tentacles stuck to my head,
And with green skin, I look rather queer.
It's a shock to find out that I'm now three feet tall,
And I just can't believe my ears!

I'm Sure I Was Abducted By Aliens 1
—Jonathan Morris

Fisherman—Georgia Cook

Fisherman

There's a fisherman with a fishing rod,
On his rod he has a line,
He sits upon the riverbank
And has a jolly good time.

There's a fisherman with a fishing line,
On his line he has a hook,
He sits upon the riverbank
And waves to a passing duck.

There's a fisherman with a fishing hook,
On his hook he has a worm,
He sits upon the riverbank
And watches it wriggle and squirm.

There's a fisherman with a fishing rod,
He just has a single wish,
To sit upon the riverbank
And to catch a little fish.

The fisherman packs up his fishing rod,
Every day the man returns.
It's fun to fish from the riverbank,
For everyone, except for worms.

Fisherman 1
—Georgia Cook

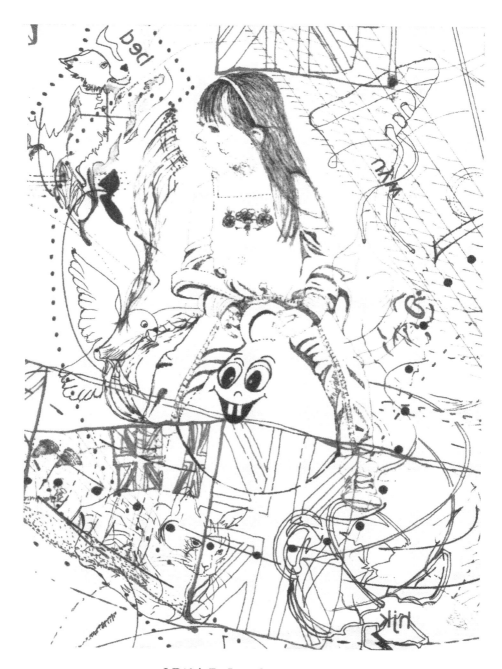

I Didn't Do It!—Carole Sherman

I Didn't Do It!

I didn't do it!
It was like that when I came.
Why is it that when stuff gets bust,
It's always me that takes the blame?

I didn't do it!
You know that sometimes things just break.
It could have been a gust of wind,
I am sure I felt an earthquake.

I didn't do it!
It was the dog; no I mean the cat;
A bird flew in and knocked it off;
When you bought it, it was like that.

I didn't do it!
But I think perhaps my friend did,
While I was upstairs doing homework,
Anyway it's easy mended.

I didn't do it!
Actually it was my sister,
If she'd not ducked, I am pretty sure
The shoe I threw would not have missed her.

I didn't do it!
Why is it you always assume
That it must be me just because,
I was the only one in the room?

I didn't do it!
Must you always put me through it?
You point an accusing finger,
But honest, Mum, I didn't do it.

First Snow—Naomi Reed

First Snow

What is this horrid white stuff
That's falling from the sky?
It's cold upon my cheek,
And stings when in my eye.
It melts upon my tongue.
I wonder whence it came,
It lies out in the garden,
And look, I wrote my name.

Ode To A Rain Cloud

Oh little black rain cloud, flying high,
You do have a silver lining,
You come along when the day's too hot,
And stop the bright sun from shining.

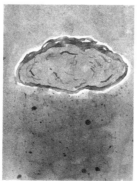

*Ode To A Rain Cloud
—Naomi Reed*

40

I'm A Boy!

I like bogies,
I like snot,
I wipe them on
My sleeve a lot.

I run around
I make a noise,
I cover floors
With all my toys.

I ride my bike
On crowded paths,
I never wash
I just hate baths.

I slide in mud,
Splash in puddles
It always seems
That I'm in trouble.

All that I do
Seems to annoy,
But it's my job,
'Cus I'm a boy!

I'm A Boy!—Claudia Swingewood-Hughes

Fetch illustrations—Robyn Johnson

Fetch—Robyn Johnson

Fetch!

"Fetch!" Yes, I can hear you, there's no need to shout,
Who's he think he is, telling me to run about?
To go chasing after balls and Frisbees and sticks,
He aught to know by now, I don't do silly tricks.

So I casually sit and look the other way,
It's a really saft game, and I don't want to play,
He can keep shouting 'fetch!' 'til he is blue in the face,
I don't care what he's thrown, I am not giving chase.

I'm not mad or an Englishman, so don't think it's fun,
To go running around in the hot midday sun.
And his other daft notion, he can bloomin' forget,
Chucking stuff in the river, 'cus I'm not getting wet.

I see all the others; they just do as they're told,
But I'm far too clever, and really too old,
The solution is simple; you'd think he would know it;
If it's something you want, then don't bloomin' throw
    it!

He's just chucked something else, and again shouted
    'Fetch'!
So I'll have a lie down, a yawn and a stretch.
As he is the one not in the best of health,
If he wants it that badly he can fetch it himself.

43

Birds Not Of A Feather—Robyn Johnson

Birds Not Of A Feather

God made me a strange kind of bird,
Though I've a beak, and wings, and more,
The others think I look absurd,
Not much like a bird at all.

Like other birds I've got feathers,
And I lay, then sit on my eggs,
Unlike most I don't care 'bout bad weather,
I've got big feet and really short legs.

So whenever I go for a stroll,
It can take a long time to get round,
And it can sometimes get really cold,
When your bum always drags on the ground.

I do not fly south for the winter,
'Cus I live there all of the time,
And flying's not something I'm in ta',
So you won't catch me even tryin'.

My wings are too skinny and stubby,
I'm not lifted whenever they flap,
I'm short and really quite tubby,
So my aerodynamics are crap.

Sometimes despair overcomes me,
I ask why I'm afflicted so,
'Cus I look really silly and clumsy,
As I waddle and slide in the snow.

Birds Not Of A Feather 1
—Robyn Johnson

Why was I not made like others?
Gracefully soaring in flight,
Or inspiring with song and bright colours,
Instead of this dull black and white.

Sometimes other birds laugh at me,
And ask why such ugliness exists,
Then they watch as I 'fly' in the sea,
And are glad God made penguins like this.

Coy Carp

If a coy carp
Met a shy shark,
I wonder which one would speak first.
Would the coy carp
Say to the shy shark,
"If we converse, shall we do it in verse?"

If a coy carp
Met a shy shark,
Would the shy shark not utter a word?
Would the coy carp
Say to the shy shark,
"I'll come closer so that you can be heard."

If a coy carp
Met a shy shark,
Would their conversation be rather dull?
'Til the shy shark
Ate the coy carp
And said, "I speak only when my mouth is full."

Coy Carp—Adam Morris

Chocolate Cake

I like to make
A chocolate cake,
With chocolate icing all around.
In the oven I bake
My chocolate cake,
'Til it's warm, and soft, and brown.

The moment I wake,
I eat chocolate cake,
All day, at my cake, I pick.
Mum says, "Don't take,
So much chocolate cake
It's going to make you sick."

But I partake
Of more chocolate cake,
'Til I'm full, right to the brim.
Mum says,
   "Your brother Jake,
   "Eats chocolate cake,
   "Look at the size of him!"

So my chocolate cake
I now forsake,
No more of it will I scoff.
Now when I make
A chocolate cake,
I just lick the icing off.

Chocolate Cake—Jonathan Morris

Dogs Are Smelly

Dogs are really smelly,
They're dirty and they stink,
Dogs are really horrible,
At least that's what I think.

Dogs are rather stupid,
Yes dogs are barking mad,
They really are the worst pet
Anybody ever had.

Dogs are just annoying,
They're barking all the time,
They sit out in their garden,
And yap, and howl, and whine.

Dogs Are Smelly—Jonathan Morris

Dogs are just big flea-bags,
They roll about in poo,
They are quite disgusting,
I'd not stroke one if I were you.

You have to take them walkies,
They chew settees and chairs,
They dig holes in your garden,
You get covered in dog hairs.

Dogs always want attention,
They're such high maintenance,
They're not bothered with hygiene,
With their 'canine fragrance'.

Yes, dogs are really smelly,
So what do you think of that?
Want a pet? Don't get a dog!
Have a pet like me; a cat.

Fairies In My Garden

I've got fairies in my garden,
They meet there every night,
They're really quite a nuisance,
And not at all polite.

They come out in the moonlight,
And dance amongst the flowers,
They drink and get quite bawdy,
Sometimes they go on for hours.

They climb and fall from trees,
Ride bikes across the lawn,
I'm fed up with their antics,
When they keep it up 'til dawn.

Yes, the bottom of my garden,
Is like a fairy glen,
I just looked out the window,
And the blighters are there again.

Last night I went right down there,
Told them, "Pick up your fairy stuff,
And clear off out my garden."
They said, "Alright mate, fair-e-nuff."

But tonight they're back again,
It seems that fairies, you can't trust,
They're down there weeing in plant pots
And spraying the dog with fairy-dust.

So I'm writing to the council,
To try and get those fairies banned,
If not, me and my wife Tinkerbelle
Are moving out of Fairyland.

Fairies In My Garden
—Robyn Johnson

Do Wasps Ever Cry?

When wasps are upset do you think that they cry?
As they watch a sad film, or their favourite pets die.
I've never seen one blubber, I cannot deny,
But I wonder, do wasps ever cry?

When they're hurt or in pain do they shed a few tears?
When they get tattoos or pierce little wasp ears.
When dumped by a girl they've loved for years,
I wonder, do wasps ever cry?

Do their eyes start to fill when they fall out of trees?
When they run and trip and take the skin off their
   knees?
Or somebody says they're not as cuddly as bees,
I wonder, do wasps ever cry?

Do they watch in despair when life gets a bit grim?
When a mate lands on a glass, slips and falls in,
And as he goes under shouts, "Help, I can't swim!"
I wonder, do wasps ever cry?

Do they ask at picnics, why they've had no invite?
And buzzing round ice-creams, no one gives them a
   bite?
When people just swat them and are none too polite,
I wonder, do wasps ever cry?

Do they sob when they're lonely, and try to pretend,
That people *don't* hate them and they *do* have a friend,
And it's *not* their fault they've a sharp pointy end,
I wonder, do wasps ever cry?

Do baby wasps blart when they're left all alone,
When Mummy and Daddy, off to work have just
   flown?
A pileup on a web means they're not coming home.
I wonder, do wasps ever cry?

When their face hits a window, as they're buzzing by,
They find no escape, though all day they will try,
When at last they expire, is there a tear in their eye?
Yes I wonder, do wasps ever cry?

Do Wasps Ever Cry?—Sue Morris

It's Scary

It's scary when you're alone at night,
When your mum turns off your bedroom light,
Beneath the bedclothes you cower in fright,
'Cus it's scary on your own.

It's creepy, with darkness all around,
It seems to echo the slightest sound,
Nowhere can sanctuary be found,
It's scary on your own.

You shiver when a cold wind blows,
Windows rattle and doors slowly close,
The moonlight creeps on tippy-toes,
It's scary on your own.

It's spooky when the shadows fall,
When neon lights dance on your wall,
And you hear the distant werewolf's call,
It's scary on your own.

It's Scary—Adam Morris

The plumbing sighs, the floorboards creak,
It seems the house is trying to speak,
You hide your face, you dare not peek,
It's scary on your own.

All night you hear things that bump about,
You want to scream. You want to shout,
"Mum please come and chase the monsters out!
It's scary on your own!"

You hear a step upon the stair,
The door creaks open, someone's there!
Your brother whispers, "Please can we share?
It's scary on your own!"

Not To Be Sneezed At

I have heard it said that the sneeze,
Is a thing of such awesome power,
The stuff comes out of your hooter
At over a hundred miles an hour.
So when you are sniffing the flowers,
Take care that, if you ever sneeze,
You do not scatter the petals,
And do not splatter the bees.
'Cus you'll find that most bumble-bees
Tend not to like it a lot,
When their flower is blown to pieces
And they are shot-blasted with snot.
They will fly off in quite a rage,
And later, think it is funny,
In hive when they get their own back,
As they make snot-flavoured honey.

Not To Be Sneezed At—Jonathan Morris

Horseradish—Jon Shariat

Horseradish

Horseradish is reddish,
Can be hot, and of course,
Remains unrelated
To any kind of horse.

What Use Are Wasps?

Does anyone know what use wasps are?
In your garden, what do they do?
I've not seen them pollinate flowers,
Or make honey: well have you?

They don't get invited to picnics,
But one always turns up without fail,
With his 'what's yours is mine' wasp attitude,
And waving his sharp, pointy tail.

He will land right on your jam sandwich,
Help himself to a mouthful or two,
Then sit there while he slowly chews it,
If you're lucky, that's all he will do,

Then his mates will turn up by the buzz load,
A huge swarm bringing panic and fear,
They will dive-bomb you while you are eating,
And swim in your pop and your beer.

They're nothing like bees, which are useful
And seem so laidback and gentle.
Wasps are aggressive, and 'in your face',
If you ask me, I think wasps are mental.

They may try and copy what bees do,
I know their game, they don't fool me.
They may be painted the same colours,
But a wasp is just a wanna-bee.

What Use Are Wasps?
—Adam Morris

Tomato

Is he a vegetable,
Or is he fruit?
Hanging about in
His shiny red suit.
When ripe for the plucking
In his ruddy getup,
I picked him and squashed him
And now he's ketchup.

Tomato—Adam Morris

Ode To A Butterfly

Oh butterfly,
You flutter by
And land upon my tablecloth.
It's soon quite clear,
When holes appear,
You're no butterfly; you're a moth!

Ode To A Butterfly—Adam Morris

Where Do Farts Go?—Claudia Swingewood-Hughes

Where Do Farts Go?

Where is it that farts go to,
When they at last make their escape?
Do they just dissolve into nothing,
Or keep their distinctive shape?

Where is it that farts go to?
Do they get together somewhere?
If you lift up a rock or a stone,
Will you find some lurking there?

Where is it that farts go to?
Do they zoom off like a rocket?
Do they like to follow folks around,
Or hang about in pockets?

Where is it that farts go to?
Is there a fart heaven or hell?
Do they have somewhere special to go,
Or lie there wherever they fell?

Where is it that farts go to?
Do they cling to the branches of trees?
Do they wait for strong passing winds,
Then surf on the crest of a breeze?

Where is it that farts go to?
Do they sit in the corners of rooms?
Or float right up to the ozone,
Like some see-through hot-air balloons?

Where is it that farts go to?
Do they gather in very large crowds
To just drift about, blotting out the sun,
In big stinky fluffy fuff-clouds?

Where is it that farts go to?
Scientists have searched high and low,
They've done research but have to admit,
The bottom line is, they don't know.

Turtle-neck Sweater

Last Christmas my Gran went to the zoo,
With a gift she'd made for the giraffe,
When the keeper got the paper off,
He said, "'Ere, are you having a laff?"

She said, "The animals must get cold,
And they should really dress a lot better,
I thought the giraffe might get a cold neck,
So I've made him this turtle-neck sweater."

Turtle-neck Sweater 1
—Jon Shariat

The keeper said, "Well, it's a mighty fine thing,
You must have used a whole lot of wool.
But how the heck will we get it on him?"
She said, "Just stick his head in, and pull."

Well it took four keepers all afternoon,
But at last they said that it fitted,
So Gran went off and bought loads more wool,
Then sat with her needles and knitted.

She sat and knitted all kinds of strange things,
Like a snood that she made for the lion,
And two pairs of trunks for the polar bear,
One to swim in, while the other was dryin'.

For the flamingos she made leggings,
Balaclavas for all the gnu,
Tea-cosies for the humps on the camels,
And woolly jumpers for the kangaroos.

The millipede got a few dozen socks,
For the crocodiles she made woolly hats,
Scarves for the pythons, the monkeys got gloves,
And the man-eating tigers, cravats.

They've said to Gran, "Please don't knit more,
Getting woollen things on animals is tough.
The gorillas won't wear their cardigans,
And the elephants hate ear muffs."

So this Christmas Gran's not knitting,
She's upset that the keepers got funny.
The animals won't get knitted gifts,
Gran says this year she'll just give them money.

Turtle-neck Sweater—Jon Shariat

November

No jumper,
No coat,
November,
No joke!

November—Naomi Reed

Never Kiss A Monkey

You should never kiss a monkey,
Or cuddle a killer whale,
Have a laugh with hyenas,
Or lie on a lion's tail.

Don't double-cross a zebra
Never take away an adder,
Don't rattle an angry rattlesnake
Or take snakes up a ladder.

Don't try and cheat a cheetah
'Cus he's better at it than you
Don't marry a black widow spider,
(The name gives you a clue!)

You should not dance with flamingos,
Never boar a wild pig,
Don't ask liar birds anything
Or give bald eagles a wig.

Make sure you know the difference
Between a moose and a mouse,
Get the wrong one as a pet,
It will tend to wreck your house.

Don't put milk out for a catfish,
Or mock a mocking bird,
And you shouldn't kiss a monkey,
Well at least that's what I've heard.

Never Kiss A Monkey
—Georgia Cook

My Father's Lit A Fire

Well my father's lit a fire,
And I really can't believe
That my father's lit a fire,
'Cus he knows it's Christmas Eve!
How does he think that Santa can
Climb the chimney with his sack?
He'll get so far and burn his bum,
Then turn round and just climb back.

Oh my father's lit a fire,
And he doesn't seem to care
That Santa Clause might burn his hat,
Melt his boots or singe his hair.
Yes my father's lit a fire,
Ignores me when I complain,
That he will ruin Christmas, 'cus
Santa won't come here again.

Yes my father's lit a fire,
And just pats me on my head,
He tells me not to worry,
And it's time I was in bed.
I say, "Well what's the point?
Tomorrow is Christmas Day,
And that rotten fire you've lit
Will scare Santa Claus away."

My Father's Lit A Fire
—Adam Morris

Oh my father lit a fire,
I think he did it just for spite.
Yes my father lit a fire,
All last night it was alight.
I wake up Christmas Morning
And I think my father's mean,
But then I change my mind because
I can see that Santa's been!

How Does Santa Do It?

I wonder how does Santa do it?
Get around the whole world so quick.
Is he just a bloke who's very fast,
Or is it some kind of 'time warp' trick?

How does he fit all of the toys in
That one tiny reindeer sleigh?
And how does he find all the houses?
Has he got a Santa Nav to help find his way?

How does he get to all the children
On one single Christmas Eve night?
Has his reindeer sleigh been supercharged,
So it can exceed the speed of light?

Is there more than just one Santa?
Does he get any help from his elves?
Does he get a load of mums and dads
To deliver the presents themselves?

No, there is only one Santa Claus,
Christmas Eve, he works all night through it,
He delivers to every boy and girl,
Still I wonder, how does Santa do it?

How Does Santa Do It?
—Adam Morris

About The Poet

Mogs (aka John Morris) has lived in the Black Country all of his life. Originally from Halesowen, where he was educated at the local grammar school, he now lives in Stourbridge with his lovely wife Sue. His two sons, Jonathan and Adam, live locally.

After leaving school Mogs worked in IT for 30 years before taking early retirement due to failing eyesight.

Mogs started writing what he refers to as 'rather dull poetry' many years ago when he was a teenager. Luckily his poems are now a lot more cheerful. He is a member of three writing groups and regularly performs at various open mic events.

http://johnnymogs.co.uk/

Acknowledgements

I would like to thank all of the people who have made this book possible, in particular those who have produced the amazing illustrations. These are:

Sue Morris
Jonathan Morris
Adam Morris,
Carole Sherman
Many thanks to the students of Stourbridge College Art and Design Centre:
Robyn Johnson
Jon Shariot
Naomi Reed
Claudia Swingewood-Hughes
Georgia Cook
Seth Milne

Also many thanks to the staff at the college, especially Department Manager Nellie Davies and tutor Simon Muttitt for all of their help and hard work.

Thanks also to the members of The Worcester Writers' Circle, Coachhouse Writers and Robin Woods Writers for their support and encouragement.

Many thanks to Mark Billen for his help and for coming up with the title *Poems Your Parents Won't Like*.

Special thanks to Ruby Sidaway for the expert and insightful opinion of a 10-year-old, which at the end of the day is the opinion that matters most.

Finally, thanks to Black Pear Press for publishing this book and to you, the reader, for reading it.

Mogs

Lightning Source UK Ltd.
Milton Keynes UK
UKHW051124190821
389065UK00003B/21